ARABEL'S RAVEN

The first story about Arabel and her pet raven Mortimer. In *Arabel's Raven* Mr Jones, while driving his taxi, notices something bedraggled in the road. Being a kind man Mr Jones stops and discovers an injured raven. Not knowing the consequences the good man takes the raven home and his four-year-old daughter Arabel falls in love at first sight. "His name is Mortimer" she announces and Mortimer has found a home. A series of thefts and a robber squirrel are only two of the dramas in this delightful tale in which Mortimer and Arabel find their way straight to our hearts.

OTHER BOOKS BY JOAN AIKEN

WITH QUENTIN BLAKE

Mortimer and Sword Excalibur
BBC Paperback

Mortimer's Portrait on Glass
BBC Paperback

Mortimer's Cross
BBC Paperback

The Winter Sleepwalker
Red Fox

OTHERS

Fox Hound, Wind Cat, Sea Mice
Hodder

Moon Cake
Hodder

The Shadow Guest
Red Fox

Tale of a One Way Street
Red Fox

The Jewel Seed
Hodder

The Cockatrice Boys
Puffin

Joan Aiken

Arabel's Raven

ILLUSTRATED BY QUENTIN BLAKE

BARN OWL BOOKS

First published in Great Britain 1972
by the British Broadcasting Corporation
35 Marylebone High Street, London W1M 4AA
This edition first published 2001 by Barn Owl Books,
157 Fortis Green Road, London N10 3LX
Barn Owl Books are distributed
by Frances Lincoln

ISBN 1 903015 14 6

A CIP catalogue record for this book
is available from the British Library

Designed and typeset by Douglas Martin
Printed in China

For Elise

Chapter One

On a stormy night in March, not long ago, a
respectable taxi-driver named Ebenezer Jones
found himself driving home, very late, through the
somewhat wild and sinister district of London
known as Rumbury Town. Mr Jones was passing
the long, desolate piece of land called Rumbury
Waste, when, in the street not far ahead, he
observed a large, dark, upright object. It was
rather smaller than a bag of golfclubs, but bigger
than a motorway cone, and it was moving slowly
from one side of the street to the other.

Mr Jones had approached to within about
twenty yards of this object when a motor-cyclist,
with a pillion passenger, shot by him at a reckless
pace and cutting in very close. Mr Jones braked
sharply, looking in his rear-view mirror. When he
looked forward again he saw that the motor-cyclist
must have struck the upright object in passing, for

it was now lying on its side, just ahead of his front wheels.

He brought his taxi to a halt. "Not but what I daresay I'm being foolish," he thought. But you can't see something like that happen without stopping to have a look."

He got out of his cab.

What he found in the road was a large black bird, almost two feet long, with a hairy fringe round its beak. At first he thought it was dead. But as he got nearer, it opened one eye slightly, then shut it again.

"Poor thing; it's probably stunned," thought Mr Jones.

His horoscope in the *Taxi Drivers' Herald* that morning had said, "Due to your skill, a life will be saved today." Mr Jones had been worrying as he drove home, because up till now he had not, so far as he knew, saved any lives that day, except by avoiding pedestrians recklessly crossing the road without looking.

"This'll be the life I'm due to save," he thought. "Must be, for it's five to midnight now," and he went back to his cab for the bottle of brandy and teaspoon he always carried in the tool-kit in case lady passengers turned faint.

It's not at all easy to give brandy to a large bird lying unconscious in the road. After five minutes there was a good deal of brandy on the cobbles, and some up Mr Jones's sleeve, and some in his shoes, but he could not be sure that any had actually gone down the bird's throat. The difficulty was that he needed at least three hands: one to hold the bottle, one to hold the spoon, and one to hold the bird's beak open. If he prised open the beak with the handle of the teaspoon, it was sure to shut again before he had time to reverse the spoon and tip in some brandy.

Suddenly a hand fell on Mr Jones's shoulder.

"Just what do you think you're doing?" inquired one of two policemen who had left their van and were standing over him.

The other sniffed in a disapproving manner. Mr Jones straightened slowly.

"I was just giving some brandy to this rook," he explained. He was rather embarrassed, because he had spilt such a lot of the brandy.

"Rook? That's no rook," said the officer who had sniffed, "That's a raven. Look at its hairy beak."

"Whatever it is, it's stunned," said Mr Jones. "A motorbike hit it."

"Ah," said the second officer, " that'll have been one of the pair who just pinched thirty thousand quid from the bank in the High Street. It's the

Cash-and-Carat boys – that ones who've done a
lot of burglaries round here lately. Did you see
which way they went?"

"No," said Mr Jones, tipping up the raven's
head, " but they'll have a dent on their bike. Could

one of you hold the bottle for me?"

"You don't want to give him brandy. Hot sweet tea's what you want to give him."

"That's right," said the other policeman. "And an ice-pack under the back of his neck."

"Burn feathers in front of his beak."

"Slap his hands."

"Undoe his shoelaces."

"Put him in the fridge."

"He hasn't got any shoelaces," said Mr Jones, not best pleased at all this advice. "If you aren't going to hold the bottle, why don't you go on and catch the blokes that knocked him over?"

"Oh, *they'll* be well away by now. Besides, they carry guns. We'll go back to the station," said the first policeman. "And you'd better not stay here, giving intoxicating liquor to a bird, or we might have to take you in for loitering in a suspicious manner."

"I can't just leave the bird here in the road," said Mr Jones.

"Take it with you then."

"Can't you take it to the station?"

"Not likely," said the second policeman. "No facilities for ravens there."

They stood with folded arms, watching, while Mr Jones slowly picked up the bird and put it in his taxi. And they were still watching as he started up and drove off.

So that was how Mr Jones happened to take the raven back with him to Number Six, Rainwater Crescent, N.W.3½, on a windy March night.

When he got home, nobody was up, which was not surprising, since it was after midnight. He would have liked to wake his daughter Arabel, who was fond of all birds and animals. But since she was quite young – she hadn't started school yet – he thought he had better not. And he knew he must not wake his wife Martha, because she had to be at work at Round & Round, the music shop in the High Street, at nine in the morning.

He laid the raven on the kitchen floor, opened the window to give it air, put on the kettle for hot sweet tea, and, while he had the match lit, burned a feather-duster under the raven's beak. Nothing happened, except that the smoke made Mr Jones cough. He saw no way of slapping the raven's hands or undoing its shoelaces, so he took some ice-cubes and a jug of milk from the fridge. He left the fridge door open because his hands were full, and anyway it usually swung shut by itself. With great care he slid a little row of ice-cubes under the back of the raven's neck.

The kettle boiled and he made the tea: a spoonful for each person and one for the pot, three in all. He also spread himself a slice of bread and fish-paste because he didn't see why he shouldn't have a little something as well as the bird. He poured out a cup of tea for himself and an egg-cupful for the raven, putting plenty of sugar in both.

But when he turned round, egg-cup in hand, the raven had gone.

"Bless me," Mr Jones said, "there's ingratitude for you! After all my trouble! I suppose he flew out of the window; those ice-cubes certainly did the trick quick. I wonder if it would be a good notion to carry some ice-cubes with me in the cab? I could put them in a vacuum-flask – might be better than brandy if lady passengers turn faint . . ."

Thinking these thoughts he finished his tea (and the raven's; no sense in leaving it to get cold), turned out the light, and went to bed.

In the middle of the night he thought, "Did I put the milk back in the fridge?"

And he thought, "No, I didn't."

And he thought, "I ought to get up and put it away."

And then he thought, "It's a cold night, the milk's not going to turn between now and breakfast. Besides, Thursday tomorrow, it's my early day."

So he rolled over and went to sleep.

Every Thursday Mr Jones drove the local fishmonger, Mr Finney, over to Colchester to buy oysters at five in the morning. So, early next day, up he got, off he went. Made himself a cup of tea, finished the milk in the jug, never looked in the fridge.

An hour after he had gone, Mrs Jones got up and put on the kettle. Finding the milk jug empty she went yawning to the fridge and pulled the door open, not noticing that it had been prevented from shutting properly by the handle of a burnt feather-duster which had fallen against the hinge. But she noticed what was inside the fridge all right. She let out a shriek that brought Arabel running downstairs.

Arabel was little and fair with grey eyes. She was wearing a white nightdress that made her look like a lampshade with two feet sticking out from the bottom. One of the feet had a blue sock on.

"What's the matter, Ma? she said.

"There's a great awful *bird* in the fridge!" sobbed Mrs Jones. "And its eaten all the cheese and a blackcurrant tart and five pints of milk and a bowl of dripping and a pound of sausages. All that's left is the lettuce."

"Then we'll have lettuce for breakfast," said Arabel.

But Mrs Jones didn't fancy lettuce that had spent the night in the fridge with a great awful bird. "And how are we going to get it out of there?"

"The lettuce?"

"The *bird*!" said Mrs Jones, switching off the kettle and pouring hot water into a pot without any tea in it.

Arabel opened the fridge door, which had swung shut. There sat the bird, among the empty milk bottles, but he was a lot bigger than they were. There was a certain amount of wreckage around him – torn foil, and cheese wrappings, and

milk splashes, and bits of pastry, and crumbs of
dripping, and rejected lettuce leaves. It was like
Rumbury Waste after a picnic Sunday.

Arabel looked at the raven, and he looked back
at her.

"His name's Mortimer," she said.

"No it's not, no it's not!" cried Mrs Jones,
taking a loaf from the bread bin and absent-
mindedly running the tap over it. "We said you
could have a hamster when you were five, or a
puppy or a kitten when you were six, and of
course call it what you wish, oh my *stars*, look at
that creature's toenails, if nails they can be called,
but not a bird like that, a great hairy awful thing
eating us out of house and home, as big as a fire
extinguisher and all black –" But Arabel was
looking at the raven and he was looking back at
her. "His name's Mortimer," she said. And she put
both arms round the raven, not an easy thing to
do, all jammed in among the milk bottles as he
was, and lifted him out.

"He's very heavy," she said, and set him down
on the kitchen floor.

"So I should think, considering he's got a
pound of sausages, a bowl of dripping, five pints of

milk, half a pound of New Zealand cheddar, and a blackcurrant tart inside him," said Mrs Jones. "I'll open the window. Perhaps he'll fly out."

She opened the window. But Mortimer did not fly out. He was busy examining everything in the kitchen very thoroughly. He tapped the table legs with his beak – they were metal, and clinked. Then he took everything out of the waste bin – a pound of peanut shells, two empty tins, and some

jam tart cases. He particularly liked the jam tart cases, which he pushed under the lino. Then he walked over to the fireplace – it was an old-fashioned kitchen – and began chipping out the mortar from between the bricks.

Mrs Jones had been gazing at the raven as if she were under a spell, but when he began on the fire-place, she said, "*Don't* let him do that!"

"Mortimer," said Arabel, "we'd like you not to do that, please."

Mortimer turned his head right round on its black feathery neck and gave Arabel a thoughtful, considering look. Then he made his first remark, which was a deep, hoarse, rasping croak.

Chapter Two

"Kaark."

It said, as plainly as words: "Well, all right, I won't do it this time, but I make no promise that I won't do it *some* time. And I think you are being unreasonable."

"Wouldn't you like to see the rest of the house, Mortimer?" said Arabel. And she held open the kitchen door. Mortimer walked – he never hopped – very slowly through into the hall, and looked at the stairs. They seemed to interest him greatly. He began going up them hand over hand – or rather, beak over claw.

When he was halfway up, the telephone rang. It stood on the window-sill and Mortimer watched as Mrs Jones came to answer it.

Mr Jones was ringing from Colchester to ask if his wife wanted any oysters.

"Oysters!" she said. "That bird you left in the

fridge has eaten sausages, cheese, dripping, black-currant tart, drunk five pints of milk, now he's chewing the stairs, and you ask if I want oysters? Perhaps I should feed him caviare as well?"

"Bird I left in the fridge?" Mr Jones was puzzled. "What bird, Martha?"

"That great black crow, or whatever it is. Arabel calls it Mortimer and she's leading it all over the house and now it's taken all the spools of cotton from my sewing drawer and is pushing them under the doormat."

"Not *it*, Ma. *He*. Mortimer," said Arabel, going to open the front door and take the letters from the postman. But Mortimer got there first, and received the letters in his beak.

The postman was so startled that he dropped his whole sack of mail in a puddle and gasped: "Nevermore will I stay later than half-past ten at the Oddfellows Ball or touch a drop stronger than Caribbean lemon, *nevermore*!"

"Nevermore," said Mortimer, pushing two bills and a postcard under the doormat. Then he retrieved the postcard again by spearing it clean through the middle. Mrs Jones let out a wail.

"Arabel, *will* you come in out of the street in

your nightie! Look what that bird's done, chewing up the gas bill. Nevermore, indeed! I should just about say it *was* nevermore. No I don't want any oysters, Ebenezer Jones, and please shut the front door and *stop* that bird from pushing all those plastic flowers under the stair-carpet."

Mr Jones couldn't understand all this, so he rang off. Five minutes later the telephone rang again. This time it was Mrs Jones's sister Brenda, to ask if Martha would like to play bingo that evening. But this time Mortimer got to the phone first; he picked up the receiver with his claw, exactly as he had seen Mrs Jones do, delivered a loud clicking noise into it – *click* – and said: "Nevermore!"

Then he replaced the receiver.

"My goodness!" Brenda said to her husband. "Ben and Martha must have had a terrible quarrel; he answered the phone and he didn't sound a *bit* like himself!"

Meanwhile Mortimer had climbed upstairs and was in the bathroom trying the taps; it took him less than five minutes to work out how to turn them on. He like to watch the cold water running, but the hot, with its clouds of steam, for some reason annoyed him, and he began throwing things at the hot tap: bits of soap, sponges, nail-brushes, face flannels.

They choked up the plug-hole and within a short time the water had overflowed and was flooding the bathroom.

"Mortimer, I think you'd better not stay in the bathroom," Arabel said.

Mortimer was good at giving black looks; he gave Arabel a black look. But she took no notice.

She had a red truck, which had once been filled with wooden building bricks. The bricks had been lost long ago, but the truck was in good repair.

"Mortimer, wouldn't you like a ride in this red truck?"

Mortimer thought he would. He climbed into the truck and stood there waiting. Arabel took hold of the handle and started pulling him along. When Mrs Jones noticed Arabel she nearly had a fit.

"It's not bad enough that you've adopted that big, ugly, sulky bird, but you have to pull him in a truck. Don't his legs work? Why can't he walk, may I ask?"

"He doesn't feel like walking just now," Arabel said.

"Of course! And I suppose he's *forgotten* how to *fly*!"

"I *like* pulling him on the truck," Arabel said, and she pulled him into the garden. Presently Mrs Jones went off to work at Round & Round, the music shop, and Granny came in to look after Arabel. All Granny ever did was sit and knit. She liked answering the phone, too, but now every time it rang Mortimer got there first, picked up the receiver, and said: "Nevermore!"

People who rang up to order taxis were puzzled and said to one another, "Mr Jones must have retired."

They had baked beans for lunch.

Mortimer enjoyed the baked beans, but his table-manners were very light-hearted. He liked knocking spoons and forks off the table, pushing them under the rush matting, and fetching them out again with a lot of excitement. Granny wasn't so keen on this.

While Granny was having her nap, Arabel looked at comics and Mortimer looked at the stairs. There seemed to be something about the stairs that appealed to him.

When Mr Jones came home at tea-time the first thing he said was: "What's happened to the three bottom steps?"

"What has, then?" asked Granny, who was short-sighted and anyway busy spreading jam.

"They aren't there."

"It wasn't Mortimer's fault," said Arabel. "He didn't know we need the stairs."

"Mortimer? Who's Mortimer?"

Just then Mrs Jones came home.

"That bird has got to go," said Mr Jones accusingly the minute she had put down her shopping-basket and taken off her coat.

"Who's talking? *You* were the one who left him in the fridge."

Mortimer looked morose and sulky and black at Mr Jones's words. He sank his head between his shoulders and ruffled up the beard round his beak and turned his toes in as if he did not care one way or the other. But Arabel went so white that her father thought she was going to faint.

"If Mortimer goes," she said, "I shall cry *all* the time. Very likely I shall die."

"Oh well . . ." said Mr Jones. "But, mind, if he

stays, he's not to eat any more stairs!"

Just the same, during the next week or so, Mortimer did chew up six more stairs. The family had to go to bed by climbing a ladder. Luckily it was an aluminium fruit ladder, or Mortimer would probably have chewed that up too; he was very fond of wood.

There was a bit of trouble because he wanted to sleep in the fridge every night, but Mrs Jones put a stop to that; in the end he agreed to sleep in the airing-cupboard. Then there was a bit more trouble because he pushed all the soap and toothbrushes under the bathroom lino and they couldn't get the door open. The fire-brigade had to climb through the window.

"He's not to be left alone in the house," Mr Jones said. "On the days when Arabel goes to play-group, Martha, he'll have to go to work with you."

"Why can't he come to play-group with me?" Arabel asked.

Mr Jones just laughed at the question.

Mrs Jones was not enthusiastic about taking Mortimer to work with her.

"So I'm going to pull him up the High Street on that red truck? You must be joking."

"He can ride on your shopping-bag on wheels," Arabel said. "He'll like that."

At first the owners of the music shop, Mr Round and Mr Toby Round, were quite pleased to have Mortimer sitting on the counter. People who lived in Rumbury Town heard about the raven in the music shop and were curious; they came in out of curiosity, and then they played discs, and then, as often as not, bought the discs. And at first Mortimer was so astonished at the music that he sat still on the counter for hours at a time looking like a stuffed bird. At tea-time, when Arabel came home from play-group, she told him what she had been doing and pulled him around on the red truck.

But presently Mortimer became bored by just listening to the music. He took to answering the telephone and saying "Nevermore!" Then he began taking triangular bites out of the edges of discs. After that it wasn't so easy to sell them. Then he noticed the spiral stairs which led down to the classic and folk departments. One morning Mr Round and Mr Toby Round and Mrs Jones were all very busy arranging a display of new issues in the shop window. When they had finished they discovered that Mortimer had eaten the spiral staircase.

"Mrs Jones, you and your bird will have to go. We have kind, long-suffering natures, but

Mortimer has done eight hundred and seventeen pounds, sixty-seven pence' worth of damage. You may have a year to repay it. Please don't trouble to come in ever again."

"Glad I am *I* haven't such a kind, long-suffering nature," snapped Mrs Jones, and she dumped Mortimer on top of her wheeled shopping-bag and dragged him home.

"Stairs!" she said to Arabel. "What's the use of a bird who eats stairs? Gracious knows there's enough rubbish in the world – why can't he eat tonic bottles, or ice-cream cartons, or used cars, or oil slicks, tell me that? But no! he has to eat the only thing that joins the upstairs to the downstairs."

"Nevermore!" said Mortimer.

"Tell that to the space cavalry!" said Mrs Jones.

Arabel and Mortimer went and sat side by side on the bottom rung of the fruit ladder, leaning against one another and very quiet.

"When I'm grown up," Arabel said to Mortimer, "we'll live in a house with a hundred stairs and you can eat them all."

Meanwhile, since the bank raid on the night Mr Jones had found Mortimer, several more places in Rumbury Town had been burgled. Brown's, the ironmongers, and Mr Finney the fishmonger, and the Tutti-Frutti Sweetie Shoppe.

On the day after Mrs Jones left Round & Round, she found another job, at Peter Stone, the jeweller's in the High Street. She had to take both Arabel and Mortimer with her to work, since play-group was finished till after Easter, and Granny had gone to Southend on a visit. Arabel pulled Mortimer to the shop every day on the red truck. Peter Stone had no objection to their coming.

"The more people in the shop, the less chance of a hold-up," he said. "Too much we're hearing about these Cash-and-Carat boys for my taste. Raided the supermarket yesterday, they did; took a thousand tins of Best Jamaica blend coffee, as the cashbox was jammed. Coffee! What would they want with a thousand tins?"

"Perhaps they were thirsty," Arabel said. She and Mortimer were looking at their reflections in a glass case full of bracelets. Mortimer tapped the glass in an experimental way with his beak.

"That bird, now," Peter Stone said, giving Mortimer a thoughtful look, "he'll behave himself? He won't go swallowing any diamonds? That brooch he's looking at now is worth forty thousand pounds."

Mrs Jones drew herself up. "Behave himself? Naturally he'll behave himself," she said. "Any diamonds he swallows I guarantee to replace!"

A police sergeant came into the shop. "I've a message for your husband," he said to Mrs Jones. "We've found a motorbike and we'd be glad if he'd step up to the station and say if he can identify it as the one that passed him the night the bank was robbed." Then he saw Mortimer. "Is that the bird that got knocked over? *He'd* better come along as well; we can see if he fits the dent in the petrol-tank."

"Nevermore," said Mortimer, who was eyeing a large clock under a glass dome.

He'd better not talk like that to the Super," the sergeant said, "or he'll be charged with obstructing the police."

"Have they any theories about the identity of the gang?" Peter Stone asked.

"No, they always wear masks. But we're pretty sure they're locals and have a hideout somewhere in the district, because we always lose track of them so fast. One odd feature is that they have a very small accomplice, about the size of that bird there," the sergeant said, giving Mortimer a hard stare.

"How do you know?"

"When they robbed the supermarket, someone

got in through the manager's cat-door and opened a window from inside. If birds had fingerprints," the sergeant said, "I wouldn't mind taking the dabs of that shifty-looking fowl. *He* could get through a cat-door easy enough."

"Your opinions are uncalled-for," said Mrs Jones. "Thoughtless our Mortimer may be, untidy at times, but honest as a doughnut I'll have you know. And the night the supermarket was robbed he was in our airing-cupboard, with his head tucked under his wing."

"I've known some doughnuts not all they should be," said the sergeant.

"Kaaark," said Mortimer.

Chapter Three

Five minutes after the sergeant had gone, Peter Stone went off for his lunch.

And five minutes after *that*, two masked men walked into the shop.

One of them pointed a gun at Mrs Jones and Arabel, the other smashed a glass case and took out the diamond brooch which Peter Stone had said was worth forty thousand pounds.

Out of the gunman's pocket clambered a grey squirrel with an extremely villainous expression. It looked hopefully round the shop.

"Piece of apple-pie, this job," said the masked man who had taken the diamond brooch. "We'll give Sam the brooch and he can use the bird to hitch a ride to our pad. Then if the cops should stop us, they can't pin anything on us."

Mortimer, who was eating one of the cheese sandwiches Mrs Jones had brought for her lunch,

suddenly found a gun jammed against his ribs.
The squirrel jumped on his back.

"You'd better co-operate, Coal-face," the
gunman said. "This is a flyjack. Fly where Sam
tells you, or you'll be blown to forty bits. Sam

carries a bomb round his neck on a shoelace; all he has to do is pull out the pin with his teeth.

"Oh, please don't blow up Mortimer," Arabel said to the gunman. "I think he's forgotten how to fly."

"He'd better remember pretty fast."

"Oh dear, Mortimer, perhaps you'd better do what they say."

With a creak that could be heard all over the jeweller's shop, Mortimer unfolded his wings and, to his own surprise as much as anyone else's, flew out through the open door. The two thieves walked calmly after him.

As soon as they were gone, Mrs Jones went into hysterics, and Arabel rang the alarm buzzer.

In no time a police-van bounced to a stop outside, with siren screaming and lights flashing. Peter Stone came rushing back from the Fish Bar.

Mrs Jones was still having hysterics, but Arabel said: "Two masked gunmen stole a diamond brooch and gave it to a squirrel to carry away and he's flown off on our raven. Please get him back!"

"Where did the two men go?"

"They just walked off up the High Street."

"All sounds like a fishy tale to me," said the police sergeant – it was the same one who had been in earlier. "You sure you didn't just give the brooch to the bird and tell him to flit off with it to the nearest stolen-property dealer?"

"Oh, how could you say such a thing," wept

Mrs Jones, "when our Mortimer's the best-hearted raven in Rumbury Town?"

"Any clues?" said the sergeant to his men.

"There's a trail of cheese-crumbs here," said the constable. "We'll see how far we can follow them."

The police left, following the trail of cheese, which led all the way up Rumbury High Street, past the bank, past the fishmonger, past the super-market, past the ironmonger, past the music shop, past the war memorial, and stopped at the tube station.

"He's done us," said the sergeant. "Went on by tube. Did a large black bird buy a ticket anywhere about ten minutes ago?" he asked Mr Gumbrell, the booking clerk.

"No."

"He could have got a ticket from a machine," one of the constables pointed out.

"They all say *Out of Order*."

"Anyway, why should a bird buy a ticket? He could just fly into a train," said another constable. "Maybe the girl's telling the truth."

All the passengers who had travelled on the Rumberloo Line that morning were asked if they had seen a large, black bird carrying a diamond brooch. None of them had.

"No offence, Mrs Jones," said Peter Stone, "but in these doubtful circumstances I'd just as soon you didn't come back after lunch. We'll say nothing about the forty thousand pounds for the brooch at present. Let's hope the bird is caught with it on him."

"He didn't take it," said Arabel. "You'll find out."

Arabel and Mrs Jones walked home to Number Six, Rainwater Crescent. Arabel was pale and silent, but Mrs Jones scolded all the way.

"Any bird with a scrap of gumption would have taken the brooch off that wretched little rat of a squirrel. Ashamed of himself, he ought to be! Nothing but trouble and aggravation we've had since Mortimer has been in the family; let's hope that's the last of him."

Arabel said she didn't want any tea, and went to bed, and cried herself to sleep.

That evening Mr Jones went up to the police station and identified the motorbike as the one that had passed him the night the bank had been robbed.

"Good," said the sergeant. "We found a couple

of black feathers stuck to a bit of grease on the tank. If you ask *me*, that bird's up to his beak in all this murky business."

"How could he be?" Mr Jones said. "He was just crossing the road when the bike went by."

"Maybe they slipped him the cash as they passed."

"In that case we'd have seen it, wouldn't we? Do you know who the bike belongs to?"

It was found abandoned on the Rumberloo Line embankment, where it comes out of the tunnel. We've a theory, but I'm not telling *you*; your family's under suspicion. Don't leave the district without informing us."

Mr Jones said he had no intention of leaving. "We want Mortimer found. My daughter's very upset."

Arabel was more than upset, she was in despair. She wandered about the house all day, looking at the things that reminded her of Mortimer – the fireplace bricks without any mortar, the tattered hearth-rug, the plates with beak-sized chips missing, the chewed upholstery, all the articles that turned up under carpets and lino, and the missing stairs. The carpenter hadn't come yet to replace them, and Mr Jones was too dejected to nag him.

"I wouldn't have thought I'd get fond of a bird so quick," he said. "I miss his sulky black face and his thoughtful ways and the sound of him crunching about the house. Eat up your tea, Arabel dearie, there's a good girl. I expect Mortimer will find his way home by and by."

But Arabel couldn't eat. Tears ran down her nose and on to her bread and jam until it was all soggy. That reminded her of the flood that

Mortimer had caused by blocking up the bath plug, and the tears rolled even faster. "Mortimer doesn't know our address!" she said. "He doesn't even know our name!"

"We'll offer five pounds reward for his return," Mr Jones said.

"Five pounds!" cried Mrs Jones who had just come home from the supermarket where she now worked. "Five pounds you offer for the return of that black Fiend when already we owe eight hundred and seventeen pounds and sixty-seven new pence to Round & Round, let alone the forty thousand to Peter Stone?"

Just the same Mr Jones stuck up his Reward sign in the sub-post-office, alongside one from Peter Stone, offering a thousand pounds for information that might lead to the return of his brooch, and similar ones from the bank, ironmonger and fishmonger.

Meanwhile, what of Mortimer and the squirrel?

They had flown as far as the tube station. There, Sam, by kicking Mortimer in the ribs and punching the top of his head, had directed him to fly into the station entrance.

Rumbury Town Station is very old. The two entrances have big round arches with sliding openwork iron gates, and the station is faced all over with tiny raw-meat-coloured tiles. A dark-blue enamel sign says:

London General Omnibus & Subterranean
Railway Company
By appmnt. to His Majesty King Edward VII

For nearly fifty years there had been only one slow, creaking old lift to take people down to the trains. A sign on it said: *Not authorized to carry more that 12 passengers.* People too impatient to wait for it had to walk down about a thousand spiral stairs. But lately the station had been modernised by the additional of a handsome pair of escalators, one up, one down, which replaced the spiral stairs. Nothing else was modern: the ticket machines were so old that people said they would work only for a Queen Victoria bun penny; the bookstall was always shut; the chocolate machines had been empty for generations; and down below, as well as the tube platforms, there were all kinds of mysterious old galleries. In the days when trams still ran in London, Rumbury had also been an underground tramway station, connecting with the Kingsway, Aldwych and Spurgeon's Tabernacle Line.

Not many trains stop at Rumbury Town; most of them rush straight through from Nutmeg Hill to Canon's Green.

Old Mr Gumbrell, the booking clerk, was Mr Jones's uncle. Besides selling tickets, he also ran the lift. He was too short-sighted to see across to

the lift from the booking-office, so when he had
sold twelve tickets he would lock up his office and
take the lift down. This meant that sometimes
people had to wait a very long time for a lift, but it
didn't much matter as there probably wouldn't be
a train for hours. However, in the end there were
complaints, which was why the escalators were
installed. Mr Gumbrell enjoyed riding on these,
which he called escatailors; he used to leave the lift
at the bottom and travel back up the moving stairs.

He did this on the day when Mortimer and the
squirrel arrived. He ran the lift slowly down, never
noticing that Mortimer, with Sam the squirrel still
grimly clutching him, was perched high up near
the ceiling on the frame of a poster.

Mr Gumbrell left the lift at the bottom, and
sailed back up the escalator, mumbling to himself:
"Arr, these-ere moving stairs do be an amazing
wonder of science. What ever will they think of
next?"

When Mr Gumbrell got to the top again he
found the police there, examining the trail of
cheese-crumbs which stopped outside the station
entrance. They stayed a long time, but Mr
Gumbrell could give them no useful information.

"Birds and squirrels!" he muttered when they had gone. "Is it likely you'd be a-seeing birds and squirrels with di'mond brooches in a tube station?"

The phone rang. There was only one telephone in the station, a public call-box with the door missing, so if people wanted to ring up Mr Gumbrell – which did not often happen – they rang on that line.

This time it was Mr Jones.

"Is that you, Uncle Arthur?"

"O' course it's me! Who else would it be?"

"We just wondered if you'd seen Arabel's raven. The trail of cheese-crumbs led up your way, the police said."

"No I have not seen a raven," snapped Mr Gumbrell. "Coppers a-bothering here all afternoon, but still I haven't! Nor I haven't seen a Socrates bird nor a cassodactyl nor a pterowary. This is a tube station, not a zoological garden."

"Will you keep a look-out, just the same?" said Mr Jones.

Mr Gumbrell thumped back the receiver. He was fed up at all the bother. "If I wait here any longer," he said, "likely the militia and the beef-guards and the horse-eaters and the traffic wardens'll be along too. I'm closing up."

Rumbury Town Station was not supposed to be closed except between 1 a.m. and 5 a.m., but in fact Mr Gumbrell often did close it earlier if his bad toe was bothering him. No one had complained yet.

"Even if me toe ain't aching now, likely it'll start any minute with all this willocking about," Mr Gumbrell argued to himself. So he switched off the escalators, locked the lift gates and ticket office, rang up Nutmeg Hill and Canon's Green to tell them not to let any trains stop, padlocked the big main mesh gates, and stomped off home to supper.

Chapter Four

Next morning there were several people waiting to catch the first train to work when Mr Gumbrell arrived to open up. They bustled in as soon as he slid the gates back and didn't stop at the booking-office for they all had season tickets. But when they reached the top of the escalator they did stop, in dismay and astonishment.

For the escalators were not there: nothing but a big, gaping, black hole.

"Someone's pinched the stairs," said a Covent Garden porter.

"Don't be so soft. How could you pinch an escalator?" said a milkman.

"Well, they're gone, aren't they?" said a bus conductor. "What's *your* theory? Earthquake? Sunk into the ground?"

"Squatters," said a train driver. "Mark my words, squatters have taken 'em."

"How'd they get through the locked gates? Anyway, what'd they take them *for*?"

"To squat on, of course."

Mr Gumbrell stood scratching his head. "Took my escatailors," he said sorrowfully. "What did they want to go and do that for? If they'd 'a took the lift, now, I wouldn't 'a minded near as much. Well, all you lot'll have to go down in the lift, anyways – there ain't twelve of ye, so it's all right."

It wasn't all right though. When he pulled the lever that ought to have brought the lift up, nothing happened.

"And I'll tell you why," said the train driver, peering through the closed top gates. "Someone's been and chawed through the lift cable."

"Sawed through it?"

"No, kind of chewed or haggled through; a right messy job. Lucky the current was switched off, or whoever done it would have been frizzled like popcorn."

"Someone's been sabotaging the station," said the bus conductor. "Football fans, is my guess."

"Hippies, more like."

"Someone ought to tell the cops."

"Cops!" grumbled Mr Gumbrell. "Not likely!

Had enough of them in yesterday a-scavenging about for ravens and squirrels."

Another reason why he did not want the police called in was because he didn't want to admit that he had left the station unattended for so long. But the early travellers, finding they could not get a train there, walked off to the next stop down the line, Nutmeg Hill. They told their friends at work what had happened, and the story spread. Presently a reporter from the *Rambury Borough News* rang up the tube station for confirmation of the tale.

"Is that RumburyTown Station? Can you tell me, please, if the trains are running normally?"

"Nevermore!" croaked a harsh voice, and the receiver was thumped down.

"You'd better go up there and have a look round," said the editor, when his reporter told him of this puzzling conversation.

So the reporter – his name was Dick Otter – took a bus up to the tube station.

It was a dark, drizzly, foggy day, and when he peered in through the station entrance he thought that it looked like a cave inside, under the round arches: the ticket machines, with their dim little lights, were like stalagmites, the white tiled floor was like a sheet of ice, the empty green chocolate machines were like hanks of moss dangling against the walls, and old Mr Gumbrell with his white whiskers, seated inside the ticket kiosk, was like some wizened goblin with his little piles of magic cards telling people where they could go.

"Is the station open?" Dick asked.

"*You* walked in, didn't you? But you can't *go* anywhere," said Mr Gumbrell.

Dick went over and looked at the gaping hole where the moving staircases used to be. Mr Gumbrell had hung a couple of chains across, to stop people falling down.

Then Dick peered through the lift gates, and down the shaft.

Then he went back to Mr Gumbrell, who was reading yesterday's football results by the light of a candle. It was very dark in the station entrance because nearly all the light switches were down below and Mr Gumbrell could not get at them.

"Who do you think took the escalators?" Dick asked, getting out his notebook.

Mr Gumbrell had been thinking about this a good deal, on and off, during the morning.

"Spooks," he replied "Spooks what doesn't like modern inventions. I reckon this station's haunted. As I've bin sitting here this morning, there's a ghostly voice what sometimes comes and croaks in me lughole. 'Nevermore,' it says, 'nevermore.' That's one reason why I haven't informed the cops. What could they do? What that voice means is that this station shall nevermore be used."

"I see," said Dick thoughtfully. In his notebook he wrote: *Is Tube Station Haunted or is Booking Clerk Round the Bend?*

"What else makes you think it's haunted?" he asked.

"Well," said Mr Gumbrell, "there couldn't *be* anybody downstairs, could there? I locked up last night, when the nine o'clock south had gone, and I phoned 'em at Nutmeg Hill and Canon's Green not to let any trains stop here till I give 'em word again. No one would've gone down this end after that, and yet sometimes I thinks as I can hear voices down the lift shaft a-calling out '*help, help*'! Which is a condradiction of nature, since, like I said, no one could be down there."

"Supposing they'd gone down last night before

you locked up?"

"Then they'd 'a caught the nine o'clock south, wouldn't they? No, 'tis ghosties down there all right."

"Whose ghosts do you think?"

"'Tis the ghosties of they old tram-car drivers. Why do I think that? Well, you look at these-ere tickets."

Mr Gumbrell showed a pile of green tenpenny tube tickets. Each had a large triangular snip taken from one side.

"See! A ghostie did that!" he said triumphantly. "Who else could've got into my ticket office? The only way in was through the slot, see, where the passengers pays their fares. A 'yuman couldn't get through there, but a ghostie could. It was the ghostie of one of they old tram-car conductors, a-hankering to clip a ticket again like in bygone days, see? And the same ghostie pinched the ham sandwich I'd been a-saving for my breakfast and left nowt but crumbs. That's why I haven't rung Head Office, neether, 'cos what would be the use? If they did put in a pair of new escatailors, and fix the lift, the new ones'd be gone again by next day. that's what the voice means when it says

'Nevermore'."

"You think you can hear voices crying 'help, help', down the lift shaft?" Dick went and listened but there was nothing to be heard at that moment.

"Likely I'm the only man as can hear 'em," said Mr Gumbrell.

"It seems to me I can *smell* something though," Dick said, sniffing.

Up from the lift shaft floated the usual smell of tube station – a queer, warm, dusty metallic smell like powdered ginger. But as well as that there was another smell – fragrant and tantalizing. "Smells to me like coffee," Dick said.

"There you are, then!" cried Mr Gumbrell triumphantly. "They old tram-drivers used to brew up a big pot o' coffee when they was waiting for the last tram back to Brixton of a night-time."

"I'd like to get some pictures of the station," said Dick, and he went over to the call-box and dialled his office, to get a photographer. But as he waited with the coin in his hand, ready to put it in the slot when the pips went, something large and black suddenly wafted past his head in the gloom, snatched the receiver from him, and whispered harshly in his ear: "Nevermore!"

Next day the *Rumbury Borough News* had a headline: IS OUR TUBE STATION HAUNTED? And beneath: "Mr Gumbrell, ticket collector and booking clerk there for the last forty years, asserts that it is. 'Ghosts of old-time tram-car drivers sit downstairs,' he says, 'playing dominoes and drinking liquorice water.' " (Dick Otter had phoned his story from the call-box in the sub-post-office, and the girl in the newsroom had misheard "drinking coffee" as "drinking toffee", which she rightly thought was nonsense so she changed it to "drinking liquorice water.")

"Shan't be able to meet people's eyes in the street," said Mrs Jones at breakfast. "Going barmy your Uncle Arthur is, without a doubt. Haunted tube station? Take him along to see the doctor, shall I?"

The postman rang, with a letter on Recorded Delivery from a firm of lawyers: Messrs Gumme, Harbottle, Inkpen and Rule. It said:

Dear Madam,

Acting as solicitors for Mr Round and Mr Toby Round, we wish to know when it will be convenient for you to pay the eight hundred and

seventeen pounds and sixty-seven pence' worth of
damage that you owe our clients for Destruction
of Premises?

This threw Mrs Jones into a dreadful flutter.
"That I should live to see the day when we are
turned out of house and home on account of a
black fiend of a bird fetched in off the street by my
own husband and dragged about on a red wooden
truck by my own daughter!"

"Well you haven't lived to see the day yet," said
Mr Jones. "Wild creatures, ravens are counted as,
in law, so we can't be held responsible for the
bird's actions. I'll go round and tell them so, and
you'd better do something to cheer up Arabel. I've
never seen the child so thin and mopey."

He drove his taxi up to Round & Round, the
music shop, but, strangely enough, neither Mr
Round nor Mr Toby Round was to be seen; the
place was locked, silent and dusty.

After trying to persuade Arabel to eat her
breakfast – which was no use, as Arabel wouldn't
touch it – Mrs Jones decided to ring Uncle Arthur
and tell him he should see a doctor for his nerves.
She called up to the tube station, but the

telephone rang and rang and nobody answered.
(In fact the reason for this was that a great many
sightseers, having read the piece in the newspaper,
had come to stare at the station, and Mr Gumbrell
has having a fine time telling them all about the
ways of the old tram-car drivers.) While Mrs Jones
was still holding the telephone and listening to the
bell ring, another bell rang, louder: the front-door
bell.

"Trouble, trouble, nothing but trouble,"
grumbled Mrs Jones. "Here, Arabel lovey, hold
the phone and say 'Hello Uncle Arthur, Mum
wants to speak to you' if he answers, will you,
while I see who's at the front door."

Arabel took the receiver and Mrs Jones went to
the front door, where there were two policemen.
She let out a screech.

"It's no use that pair of sharks sending you to
arrest me for their eight hundred and seventeen
pounds – I haven't got it if you were to turn me
upside-down and shake me till September!"

The police looked puzzled and one of them
said, "I reckon there's some mistake? We don't
want to turn you upside-down – we came to ask
you if you recognize this?"

He held out a small object in the palm of his hand.

Mrs Jones had a close look at it.

"Why certainly I do," she said. "That's Mr Round's tie-pin – the one he had made from one of his back teeth when it fell out as he ate a plateful of Irish stew."

Meanwhile Arabel was still sitting on the half-finished new stairs holding the phone to her ear, when all at once she heard a hoarse whisper:

Arabel was so astonished she almost dropped the telephone. She looked all round her – nobody there. Then she looked back at the phone, but it had gone silent again. After a minute a different voice barked: "Who's that?"

"Hello, Uncle Arthur, it's me, Arabel, Mum wants to speak to you."

"Well, I don't want to speak to her," said Mr Gumbrell, and he hung up.

Arabel sat on the stairs and said to herself: "That was Mortimer. He must be at the tube station because that's where Uncle Arthur is."

Chapter Five

Arabel had often travelled by tube, and knew the way to the station. She got her red truck, and she put on her thick, warm, woolly coat, and she went out of the back door because her mother was still talking at the front and Arabel didn't want to be stopped. She walked up the High Street, past the bank. The manager looked out and said to himself: "That child's too young to be out on her own. I'd better follow her and find who she belongs to."

He started after her.

Next Arabel passed the supermarket. The manager looked out and said to himself: "That's Mrs Jones's little girl. I'll just nip after her and ask her where her mother's got to today." So he followed Arabel.

Then she past the Round & Round music shop, but there was nobody in it, and Mr Jones had become tired of waiting and driven off in his taxi.

Then she passed Peter Stone, the jeweller. Peter Stone saw her through the window and thought: "That girl looks as if she knows where she means to go. And she was the only one who showed any sense after my burglary. Maybe it was a true story about the squirrel and the raven. Anyway, no harm in following her to see where she goes." So he locked up his shop and followed.

Arabel passed the fire-station. Usually the firemen waved to her – they had been friendly ever since they had had to come and climb in the Joneses' bathroom window – but today they were all hastily pulling on their helmets and rushing about. And just as she had gone past, the fire-engine shot out and by her, going lickety-spit.

Presently Arabel came to the tube station. The first person she saw there was her great-aunt Annie Gumbrell.

"*Arabel Jones!* What are you doing walking up the High Street by yourself, liable to get run over and kidnapped and murdered and abducted and worse? The idea! Where's your mother? And where are you going?"

"I'm looking for Mortimer," said Arabel, and she kept on going. "I've stayed on the same side all the way; I didn't have to cross over," she said over her shoulder as she went into the tube station.

Aunt Annie had come up to the station to tell Uncle Arthur that he was behaving foolishly and had better come home, but she couldn't get near him because of the crowd. In fact Arabel was the only person who *could* get into the station entrance now, because she was so small – there was just room for her and then the place was completely crammed. Aunt Annie wasn't able to get in at all. When Arabel was inside somebody kindly picked her up and set her on top of a ticket machine so that she could see.

"What's happening?" she asked.

"They reckon someone's stuck in the lift, down at the bottom. So they're a-going to send down a fireman, and he'll go in through the trap-door in the roof of the lift and fetch 'em back," said her great-uncle Arthur, who happened to be standing by her. "I've told 'em and told 'em 'tis the ghosties of old tram drivers, but they don't take no notice."

"Why don't they just send a train from Nutmeg Hill, and get someone from it to go to see what the matter is?"

"Train drivers' union won't let 'em stop. They

say if 'tis the ghosties of old tram drivers stuck in the lift, 'tis a different union and no concern of theirs."

Now the firemen, who had been taking a careful look at the lift, asked everybody to please step out into the street to make room. Then they rigged up a light, because the station was so dark, and they brought in a hoist, which was mostly used for rescuing people who got stuck up church spires or on the roofs of burning buildings. They let down a fireman in a sling, and the whole population of Rumbury Town, by now standing in the street outside, said: "Coo!" and held its breath.

Presently a shout came from below.

"They've found someone,' said the firemen, and everybody said "Coo!" again and held their breath some more.

Just at this moment Arabel (still sitting on top of the ticket machine for she was in no one's way there) felt a thump on her right shoulder. It was lucky that she had put on her thick warm woolly coat, for two claws took hold of her shoulder with a grip like a bulldog clip. A loving croak in her ear said: "Nevermore!"

"Mortimer!" said Arabel, and she was so pleased that she might have toppled off the ticket machine if Mortimer hadn't spread out his wings

like a tightrope-walker's umbrella and balanced them both.

Mortimer was just as pleased to see Arabel as she was to see him. When he had them both balanced he wrapped his left-hand wing round her and said "Nevermore" five or six times over, in tones of great satisfaction and enthusiasm.

"Look, Mortimer, they're bringing someone up."

Slowly, slowly, up came the sling, and who should climb out but Mr Toby Round, looking hungry and sorry for himself. The minute he was landed all sorts of helpful people, St John ambulance men and stretcher-bearers and clergymen and the matron of the Rumbury General Hospital, all rushed at him with bandages and cups of tea and said, "Are you all right?"

They would have taken him away, but he said he wanted to wait for his brother.

The sling went down again at once. In a few minutes up it came with the other Mr Round. As soon as he landed he noticed Arabel and Mortimer perched on the ticket machine, and the sight of them seemed to set him in a passion.

"Grab that bird," he shouted. "*He's* the cause of

all the trouble! Gnawed through the lift cable and
ate the escalator and had my brother and me
trapped in utter discomfort for forty-eight hours!"

"And what was you a-doing down there," said
Mr Gumbrell suspiciously, "after the nine o'clock
south had come and gone?"

Just at this moment a whole van-load of police arrived with Mrs Jones, who seemed half distracted.

"*There* you are!" she screamed when she saw Arabel. "And me nearly frantic, *oh*, my goodness, there's that great awful bird, as if we hadn't enough to worry us!"

But the police swarmed about the Round brothers, and the sergeant said: "I have a warrant to arrest you two on suspicion of having pinched the cash from the bank last month and if you want to know why we think it's you that did it, it's because we found your tooth tie-pin left behind in the safe and one of Toby's fingerprints on the abandoned motorbike. And I shouldn't wonder if you did the jobs at the supermarket and the jeweller's and all the others too!"

"It's not true!" shouted Mr Toby Round. "We didn't do it! We didn't do *any* of them. We were staying with my sister-in-law at Romford on each occasion. Her name's Mrs Flossie Wilkes and she lives at two-nought-nought-one Station Approach. If you ask *my* opinion that raven is the thief –"

But the sergeant had pulled Mr Toby Round's hand from his pocket to put a handcuff on it, and, when he did so, what should come out as well but Sam the squirrel, and what should Sam be clutching in his paws but Mr Peter Stone's diamond brooch.

So everybody said "Coo!" again. And Mr Round and Mr Toby Round were taken off to Rumbury Hill police station. The police sergeant hitched a ride in the fireman's sling and went down the lift shaft and had a look round the old galleries and the disused tram station. He found the money that had been stolen from the bank, all packed in the plastic dustbins that had been stolen from Brown's the ironmongers, and he found nine hundred and ninety-nine of the thousand tins of Best Jamaica blend coffee stolen from the supermarket, and a whole lot of other things that must have been stolen from different premises all over Rumbury Town.

While he was making these exciting discoveries down below, up above Mrs Jones was saying: "Arabel, you come home directly, and don't you dare go out on your own ever again!"

"Nevermore!" said Mortimer.

So Arabel climbed down from the ticket machine, with Mortimer still on her shoulder.

"Here!" said Uncle Arthur, who had been silent for a long time, turning things over in his mind, "that bird ought to be arrested too, if he's the one what ate my escatailors and put my lift out of order! How do we know he wasn't in with those blokes and their burglaries? He was the one what helped the squirrel make off with the di'mond brooch."

He was flyjacked; he couldn't help it," said Arabel.

"Far from being arrested," said the bank manager, "he'll get a reward from the bank for helping to bring the criminals to justice."

"And he'll get one from me too." said Peter Stone.

"And from me," said the supermarket manager.

"Come along Arabel, do," said Mrs Jones, "Oh my gracious, look at the time, your father'll be home wanting his tea and wondering where in the world we've got to!"

Arabel collected her red truck, which she had left outside. and Mortimer climbed on to it.

"My stars!" cried Mrs Jones. "You're not going to pull that great, black, sulky bird all the way home on the truck when we know perfectly *well* he can fly, the lazy thing? Never did I hear anything so outrageous, never!"

"He likes being pulled," said Arabel, so that was the way they went home. The bank manager and the supermarket manager and Mr Peter Stone and quite a lot of other people saw them as far as the gate.

Mr Jones was inside and had just made a pot of tea. When he saw them come in the front gate he poured out an egg-cupful for Mortimer.

They all sat round the kitchen table and had tea. Mortimer had several egg-cupfuls, and as for Arabel, she made up for all the meals she had missed while Mortimer had been lost.

Barn Owl Books

THE PUBLISHING HOUSE DEVOTED ENTIRELY TO
THE REPRINTING OF CHILDREN'S BOOKS

RECENT TITLES

Mortimer's Bread Bin – Joan Aiken

Mortimer the raven is determined to sleep in the bread bin. Mrs Jones says no

The Spiral Stair – Joan Aiken

Giraffe thieves are about! Arabel and her raven have to act fast

Your Guess is as Good as Mine – Bernard Ashley

Nicky gets into a stranger's car by mistake

The Gathering – Isobelle Carmody

Four young people and a ghost battle with a strange evil force

Voyage – Adèle Geras

Story of four young Russians sailing to the U.S. in 1904

Private – Keep Out! – Gwen Grant

Diary of the youngest of six in the 1940s

Leila's Magical Monster Party – Ann Jungman

Leila invites all the baddies to her party and they come!

The Silver Crown – Robert O'Brien

A rare birthday present leads to an extraordinary quest

Playing Beatie Bow – Ruth Park

Exciting Australian time travel story in which Abigail learns about love

The Mustang Machine – Chris Powling

A magic bike sorts out the bullies

The Phantom Carwash – Chris Powling

When Lenny asks for a carwash for Christmas, he doesn't expect to get one,
never mind a magic one!

The Intergalactic Kitchen – Frank Rodgers

The Bird family plus their kitchen go into outer space

You're Thinking about Doughnuts – Michael Rosen

Frank is left alone in a scary museum at night

Jimmy Jelly – Jacqueline Wilson

A T.V. personality is confronted by his greatest fan

The Devil's Arithmetic – Jane Yolen

Hannah from New York time travels to Auschwitz in 1942 and acquires wisdom